THE KRAKEN

This softcover edition © 2022 by Tam O'Malley
Published by Wooden Books LLC,
San Rafael, California

First published in the UK in 2021
by Wooden Books Ltd, Glastonbury, UK

Library of Congress Cataloging-in-Publication Data
O'Malley, T.
Mythological Animals

Library of Congress Cataloging-in-Publication
Data has been applied for

ISBN-10: 1-952178-26-6
ISBN-13: 978-1-952178-26-9

Designed and typeset in Glastonbury, UK

Printed in China on 100% FSC
approved sustainable papers by FSC
RR Donnelley Asia Printing Solutions Ltd.

WOODEN
BOOKS

MYTHOLOGICAL
ANIMALS

FROM BASILISKS TO UNICORNS

Tam O'Malley

'The world is full of magic things,
patiently waiting for our senses to grow sharper'
— W.B Yeats

Page i: the Scandanavian **KRAKEN**, *after an image from St. Malo Church, France.*
Title page: Dragon chasing a **MELUSINE** (*serpent woman*) *and other beasts, Holland, 1610.*
Above: the Assyrian bull-bodied **LAMASSU** (*bull/lion, wings and human head*).

Above: A plate from Bilderbuch für Kinder, c.1800, by Friedrich Justin Bertuch, showing a variety of mythological animals, including a griffin and a mermaid.

INTRODUCTION

A NIMALS HAVE CO-EXISTED with humans since the dawn of man, so it is hardly surprising that lions, lizards, bats, wolves and even the esteemed and rarely sighted giant squid have all meandered their way into legends and lore down the centuries.

It is quite possible that sailors' fantastical tales of beguiling mermaids and sirens may be based on seals or large fish sighted at sea. The dreaded werewolf may originate in wild hairy outlaws or the deep relationship humans have enjoyed alongside man's best friend. The vampire may have its foundation in the blood-sucking vampire bat or victims of coma. Dragons may derive from giant lizards and dinosaur bones discovered at the back of ancient Chinese caves. Giant cockatrice-like flightless birds were still walking the earth only a few centuries ago.

Some mythological creatures, however, are more than murky memories. These instead take the form of powerful symbols and enduring mysteries. Ancient Mesopotamians turned to lion-headed storm demons to evoke divine interventions in society. Egyptians believed their immortality lay in the hearts of beautiful flaming firebirds. To this day, people all over the world still believe in fairies.

Whatever the truth concerning these legendary beasts of old, one thing is certain: their existence in the ageless lore of storytelling remains resolute—they are unlikely to disappear from our imaginations any time soon. So prepare to delve into some fascinating examples of these fabulous creations of myth and lore. I hope these will serve as a fine introduction to the dazzling world of MYTHOLOGICAL ANIMALS.

THE BANSHEE
foreteller of doom

THIS MOROSE, SUPERNATURAL ENTITY is mostly heard, and rarely ever seen. Known as *'the woman of the fairies'*, she haunts the chilled mists of the Irish countryside, seeking mortals under the cover of night. The BANSHEE normally appears as elderly and hag-like, more of a shadow lurking within the shadows than a ghost or apparition, but she can also resemble a mournful young woman, eyes raw and red from grief.

Her drawn, eerie, unearthly wail, a cry known as *'keening'*, portends a dreadful presage, an imminent death in the family or even the death of the witness. This sound is echoed by professional keeners, who emulate the piercing moans *'ochone'* at the wakes of funerals.

The first keening cry in Ireland was that of the Irish goddess Brighid, of the *Tuatha de Danaan*, whose wails were heard for miles around as she mourned the death of Ruadan, her only son.

Left: A Scottish Banshee, the bearer of unhoped for news in the Highlands.

Below: In her Welsh form, the Banshee is known as the Rhibyn Witch. The apparition and keening sound is said to only visit families of pure Celtic blood.

Facing page: The Bunworth Banshee, Ireland, from Croker, 1825. One modern theory is that the heart-wrenching wails of the Banshee might involve a high-frequency sound made by the soul as it prepares to leave the body, heard only by certain people.

3

Basilisk and Cockatrice

death from the eyes

The **BASILISK**, or king snake (from the Greek *basileus*, 'king'), can take a variety of forms. A small venomous snake hatched by a cockerel from the egg of a serpent or toad will grow into a winged or eight-legged serpent (*shown below*). Or, a cockerel's egg hatched by a toad 'during the days of Sirius' can produce its stunning alter-ego the **COCKATRICE** (*see opposite*). Interestingly, a cockerel's crow can kill a basilisk.

Serpents are a near-universal theme of world mythology, from the seven-hooded cosmic serpent **ANANTA SHESHA** in India to **FU XI** and **NU WA**, the male and female human-serpentine hybrids in ancient China (*see page 40*). Basilisks appear in the late Classical era on Gnostic seals as a sign of protection, whereas in the medieval period, serpents and basilisks heralded death and destruction and were a symbol of the devil.

Pliny the Elder [23–79AD] warns that, like **MEDUSA** (*see page 20*), '*Anyone who sees the eyes of a basilisk serpent dies immediately*'. Its poison is equally deadly. The basilisk burns everything in its path, creating a landscape of polluted water or desert for miles, any life or vegetation destroyed by the presence of such a poisonous entity. Middle Eastern deserts were said to owe their very creation to this destructive supernatural force. Pliny also says it could kill '*with a hiss*' and its stench could cause deadly plagues. As with Medusa, a human needed a crystal or a mirror to kill a basilisk, its own reflection being its downfall.

Left: Basilisk by Melchior Lorch, 1548. Right: Eve and the Serpent of Sin, Gunther Zainer, 1470.
By the Middle Ages the Basilisk had evolved to feature a cockerel's head, a sign of its parent bird.

Above: The Weasel and the Basilisk; engraving by Wenceslaus Hollar [1607-1677].
Weasels are immune to the murderous glance of a basilisk, and also possess a venomous bite.

BLEMMYAE AND SCIAPODS
headless and legless

BLEMMYAE were off-set humanoid monsters believed to be an ancient tribal race populating the regions of Africa, Ethiopia and Egypt. Roman writers tell of them inhabiting Upper Egypt and Nubia, where their flesh was said to taste sweet, and was much sought after. Generally docile, they were headless, their eyes and mouths instead on their chests. St Augustine witnessed some personally in Ethiopia:

> '*In this country we saw many men and women without heads, who had two great eyes in their breasts; and in countries still more south, we saw people who had but one eye in their foreheads*'. [from *Sermones ad fratres in eremo, c.1450.*]

Sir John Mandeville [1300–1371] writes of seeing them in his *Travels*, as does Sir Walter Raleigh [1552–1618] in his *Description of Guiana*.

The closely-related **SCIAPOD** or **MONOPOD** was a creature with a single, oversized foot extending from the centre of their bodies, which they used to shade themselves from the scorching Ethiopian sunshine.

Above: A plate from Sir Walter Raleigh's 1599 Brevis & Admiranda Descriptio Regni Guianae, showing Blemmyae.

Left: A Blemmyae and a Sciapod. From the Livre de Merveilles, Paris, c.1411.

Facing page: Musteros, Pigmei and Sciopedi, from Guilliano de Dati's Il Secondo Cantare dell'India, 1494. Many odd human-like creatures were believed to exist in antiquity. In his Etymologiae, c.610, Isidore of Seville describes all sorts, from pygmies to hermaphrodites.

Centaurs and Satyrs
horsemen and goatmen

The **CENTAUR** is a human-equine hybrid, a noble yet rebellious forest-dwelling beast of the ancient Thessalian mountains. **CHIRON**, first among centaurs, was celebrated as a great healer, astrologer and oracle, but other centaurs were somewhat partial to wine and rustic barbarism.

A primal race, centaurs were adept at sourcing their own food and crafting natural items, such as rocks and twigs, into weapons. Pliny describes them as man-eaters, dwelling sometimes in water. Female centaurs also exist, notably on a mural painting in Pompeii. They are closely associated with the **ONOCENTAUR**, which Isidore informs us has 'The shape of a man down to the waist, and behind has the make of an ass'.

The **SATYR** is a close relative. Greek art depicts them with the ears and tails of a horse and the legs of a horse or goat. Often found cavorting with nymphs, they were later rebranded as child-friendly **FAUNS**.

Left: Chiron teaching Achilles to play the lyre, Roman fresco from Herculaneum, 1st century AD. Below: An early depiction of fauns at play, London, c.1520.

Above: Centaur attacking a satyr, engraving by Hendrik Hondius I, Holland, c.1610. Facing page: Centaurs on the attack, illustration by Gustave Doré, for The Inferno, 1861.

CHIMERA

a great and terrible creature

The liminal **CHIMERA** (she-goat) is mentioned for the first time in Book VI of *The Iliad*, and is said to have been born in the Anatolian region of Lycia. Homer, c.850 BC, venerates this twisted daughter of **TYPHON** (*see page 48*) as being of divine stock, describing her as having a lion's head, a goat's body and a dragon's tail. The Greek poet Hesiod tells in his *Theogony*, c.700 BC, of 'A great and terrible creature, swift of foot and strong' and of the beast possessing three heads (as she often appears in 5th century bronzes). Hesiod also names **ECHIDNA**, the half-woman half-snake mate of **TYPHON**, as mother of the Chimera.

This unconquerable fire-breathing monstrosity was responsible for burning the city of Lycia to the ground, killing all within. She was eventually slain by the Corinthian hero Bellerophon, who soared high above her vomit of flames and threw a lead-tipped spear down her throat from his white winged steed **PEGASUS** (*page 21*), the melting lead choking the Chimera to death. This famous battle was widely depicted in early 7th century BC art. The true origins of the Chimera may lie within the constantly burning Mount Chimaera, a place Pliny explains 'indeed burned with a flame that does not die by day or night'.

Left: Chimera variant, Rome, 1496. Above:
Chimera, for Ulisse Aldrovandi, described c.1570.
Below: Drawing of the Chimera, Jacopo Ligozzi,
c.1600. Facing page: Genii riding on chimeras,
ornament, Hans Sebald Beham, 1544.

CYCLOPES
one-eyed giants

In Hesiod's *Theogony*, the poet tells of three **CYCLOPES**, one-eyed giants, born of Gaia by the primordial Grecian deity Ouranos. They were **BRONTES** (thunder), **STEROPES** (lightning) and **ARGES** (brightness), siblings to the mighty Titans. The three brothers were cast by their father into the grievous depths of Tartarus, before being freed and then banished again by Cronus. They were finally freed by Zeus, keen to recruit such powerful beings to fight alongside him (*upper, opposite*).

Another famous Cyclops was **POLYPHEMUS**, the leader of a cave-dwelling community of Cyclopes encountered by the hero Odysseus in Homer's *Odyssey* (*lower, opposite*). The Cyclopean walls of Mycenae, dating to c.1500 BC, were supposedly built by Cyclopes, their huge strength explaining the vast size of the stones, far too heavy to be moved by mortal men (*see tiny figure in doorway, below*).

Left: Forge of the Cyclopes, by Cornelis Cort [1533-1578]. Provided with their own forge at Mount Etna by the gods, the Cyclopes repayed Zeus for their freedom by using their fine skills in blacksmithery and metalwork. They produced a formidable range of magical weaponry for the gods to use in their campaign of war against Cronus and the Titans, including a three-pronged trident for Poseidon, Hades' helm of invisibility, Apollo's bow and arrows and the catastrophic lightning bolts with which Zeus remains most famously symbolised to this day.

Above: Polyphemus attacking the Trojan fleet, engraving by Giuseppe Maria Mitelli, 1663. In The Odyssey, Polyphemus traps Odysseus and some of his men in his cave, eating two of them for supper and another two for breakfast the next day. Odysseus escapes by blinding him.

DRAGONS
winged four-legged serpents

Colossal and serpentine of form, **DRAGONS** (from the Greek *drakon*, 'to see') are commonly depicted as highly intelligent winged and four-legged fire-breathing monstrosities, capable of both boundless loyalty and compassion and utter and reckless destruction.

Dragons feature in folklore around the globe. The immortal hundred-headed serpent **LADON** guarded the goddess Hera's Garden of the Hesperides. The Sparti soldiers sprang from dragon's teeth which King Cadmus sowed in the earth. The dragon serpent **TIAMAT** was the primordial creator goddess of ancient Babylon. The **DRAKONES AITHIOPES** were believed to be a race of large African serpents. In Hindu mythology, the Vedic serpent **VRITRA** represented the hardships of drought, holding captive all the waters of the world.

In medieval times, Satan was described as the 'Great Dragon', while ordinary dragons were known as **WORMES**. In ancient British and Welsh tradition, the treasure-seeking dragon was a symbol of courage and strength on the battlefield, hence the term **PENDRAGON** (leader in war).

European cave **OLM SALAMANDERS** were once believed to be proof of dragons, as were Indonesian **KOMODO DRAGONS** and dinosaur bones.

Above: Lung Dragon, Canton. In the Far East, dragons represent the eternal principles of the universe and supreme celestial and imperial power. The people of China consider themselves 'the children of the Dragon'. Below: The Dragons of Mount Pilatus, Athanasius Kircher, 1665.

FAIRIES

elves, goblins, pixies and gnomes

FAIRY folk across Celtic fable and legend appear as numerous entities, such as **SPRITES, LEPRECHAUNS, ELVES, GOBLINS, PIXIES** and **GNOMES**. Their name derives from the Latin *fatum*, 'fate/destiny'. Many can assume a miniature human form and wield powerful supernatural abilities which they particularly enjoy using to help or hinder human beings, depending on their famously mischievous natures.

Some say fairies exist on a higher Heavenly or Otherworldly plane, while others insist they reside here in the mortal realm. Popular in early European folklore, they may have been the first race on earth.

They are referred to as **NYMPHS** by the Greeks, **POOKAS** in Celtic mythology and **VIDYESHVARAS** in Indian folklore, and they feature in ancient tales of love and adventure in American Indian and Eskimo cultures. Across all cultures their universal mission is to guard and protect the natural world and its inhabitants, in all its forms. They often act under the guidance of a beautiful and compassionate fairy queen, **MAB** or **TITANIA** (*see Arthur Rackham's 1908 illustration opposite*).

Phosphoric light from decaying wood was often referred to as 'fairy sparks', tiny lights by which the fairy folk danced the evenings away.

GHOULS
flesh-eating zombies

GHOULS are demonic entities which lurk within graveyards and other uninhabited places. They are said to feast on the flesh of any corpses held there, before going on to possess the spirits of the deceased, preventing these poor souls from ever reaching the paradise of the afterlife. Traditionally, they were fond of drinking blood and stealing coins, and also had the ability to take on the form of their victims.

The 19th century explorer Sir Richard Burton writes of them:

'Here an ogre, a cannibal. GHULS *are rather fearsome, and do not seem to prey on humanity mearly through necessity. Their appetite is insatiable.*'

Burton gives the term for a female Ghoul, GHULAH, and explains that '*Etymologically* GHUL *is a calamity, a panic fear; and the monster is evidently the embodied horror of the grave and the graveyard*'. The word derives from the Arabic *Ghul*, meaning 'to snatch/seize', the term first appearing in English in the 1786 novel *Vathek* by William Thomas Beckford.

Ghouls hold their lurid roots in Persian, Iranian and pre-Islamic Arabian folklore. Their demonic influence is kept alive to this day, not only by isolated African and American tribes, but also throughout the world, thanks to the present-day traditions of Halloween.

Above left: 'Amina discovered with the Ghul,' from the tale of Sidi Nouman in the 1001 Nights. Above right: Child-eating Ghoul, after Father Peinard, 1894. Below: Illustration from the Mahabharata, Nepal, c. 1800, depicting the five Pandava brothers dispatching their enemy, with scavengers, vultures and ghouls in the foreground. Facing page left: Japanese Ghoul, by Katsushika Hokusai [1760-1849]. Facing page right: Shu-no-Bon, red-faced-ghoul, Edo period.

THE GORGONS

Medusa and the birth of Pegasus

The term **GORGON** derives from the ancient Greek *gorgos*, 'dreadful', and Sanskrit *garjana*, 'guttural', and relates to anything unusually hideous, especially women. The most infamous examples in classical mythology were the three monstrous winged sisters with scathing serpents for hair, **STHENO**, **EURYALE** and the terrifying **MEDUSA**. Each had vast mouths packed with sharp fangs and cruel teeth, brazen claws and large glaring eyes, and each of the sisters had only to glance at anyone unfortunate enough to cross their paths for them to be turned instantly to stone. Of the three, only Medusa was mortal.

Gorgons appear in the earliest Greek writings, including those of Homer and Pliny the Elder. Diodorus [90–30BC] believed them to be a tribe of women from Libya, who eventually met their deaths at the hands of Hercules.

According to Ovid, Medusa was once a beautiful maiden, vain of her lovely hair. But after she was assaulted by Poseidon on the steps of Athena's temple, furious Athena transformed Medusa's hair into a crawling, writhing nest of vicious snakes, '*that she may alarm her surprised foes with terror*' [*Metamorphoses iv, 792–802*, published c. 8 AD].

Left: Gorgons appear widely in Classical art. Medusa's staring contempt was used to ward off evil and protect anything it adorned.

Below: Perseus bringing Medusa's head to King Polydectes, won using the mirrored shield given to him by the gods. Two creatures sprang forth from the stump of her neck: the winged horse PEGASUS ('he who sprang') and CHRYSAOR ('the sword of gold') - both the result of Poseidon's earlier assault on Medusa.

Facing page: The Gorgons, Walter Crane, 1892.

THE GRIFFIN
emblem of valour and magnanimity

The **GRIFFIN** is '*compounded of the Eagle and the Lion, the noblest animals of their kinds*', wrote Sir Thomas Brown in 1646. It has the head, plumed wings and talons of an eagle and the burly body of a lion (*below left*). A **GYPHON** might also have the tail of a scorpion or serpent (*below right*).

Big enough to block out the sun, these daunting mountain-dwellers built sizable eyries made of pure gold. Herotodus in his *Histories*, c.440 BC, describes how in northen Scythia: "*One-eyed men called Arimaspeans steal gold from griffins*". Aelian, c.150 AD, further adds "*when prospectors approach, the griffins fear for their young, and so give battle to the intruders*".

Of Middle Eastern origin, a clear-sighted and powerful griffin could tear human beings to shreds in seconds, as well as horses and serpents. They appear in an epic poem by the Greek poet Aristeas, c.675 BC, and in Aeschylus' c.460 BC play *Prometheus Bound*. They are widely depicted in art from the ancient Babylonian, Assyrian and Persian eras. In Roman art, a mighty griffin draws the chariot of Nemesis.

Similar beasts include the Egyptian god **HORUS** (head of an eagle), **HIPPOGRIFFIN** (body of a horse), the Assyrian **LAMASSU** (body of a bull or lion, eagle's wings and human head, *see page iv*), the **LUPOGRIFFIN** (body of a dog) and the **AKHEKHU** (serpent with clawed feet).

Above: Plate from the Italian epic Orlando Furioso, *by Francesco Franceschi, illustrated in 1516 by Gustave Doré, showing the hero riding on a griffin. Could griffins have been real? Fossilized remains of the 'parrot-beaked' dinosaur Protoceratops are found in abundance along the mountainous central Asian trade routes the legendary griffin is said to have inhabited.*

Left: Middle Assyrian seal from c. 1200BC. Griffins, or Assyrian 'cloud cleaving eagles' symbolised strength, courage and protection. In Roman and Greek times, they guarded the sacred Tree of Life, the roads to salvation and the tombs of the dead. They also later became a symbol of the divine-human nature of Christ.

HARPIES AND SIRENS
an ill-omened encounter

Hideously hag-like and brandishing equally unpleasant temperaments, **HARPIES** were fierce female monsters of destruction, featuring the head and breasts of a woman and the body of a vulture or eagle. Experts of cruelty and deceit, they spread chaos, pollution and excrement wherever they ventured. A putrid, contaminating stench was a sure sign that harpies were near, said to emanate from their ever-filthy oozing underparts. Pallid of countenance and always horribly sickly-looking, they were continually tormented with unappeasable hunger.

In his *Theogony*, Hesiod relates that the harpies are the offspring of Thaumas and the Oceanid Elektra, bearing Iris (the rainbow) and the harpies **OCYPETE** (rapid) and **AELLO** (storm), later joined by **KELAINO** (the dark one). The harpy **PODARGE** (Fleetfoot) appears in *The Illiad*. In *The Quest of the Golden Fleece*, harpies vex Jason and his Argonauts and torment the blind Thracian king-seer Phineus when he sits to eat. They were eventually banished to the caverns of Mount Dikte of Crete by Zetes and Kalais, the sons of Boreas the North Wind.

Harpies are similiar in form to **FURIES** or **SIRENS**, dangerous island-dwelling women-birds who lured sailors to their deaths with their enchanting harp and lyre music and mesmerising singing. Odysseus survived his encounter with them by being tied to his ship's mast.

Above left: Sirens and **DRACONIOPIDES** *(serpent women). Above right: Harpies preventing
King Phineus from eating. Facing page: Harpies and Sirens, medieval, Sumerian and Egyptian.*

*'No monster is more grim than the Harpies: no stroke of divine wrath was ever more cruel and no
wickeder demon ever soared upwards from the waters of the Styx' (Book 3, Virgil's Aeneid)*

HYDRA AND CERBERUS
many-headed siblings

The hideous and vicious **HYDRA** lived in the steaming marshes surrounding the lake of Lerna. Its nine heads were supported on long serpentine necks, each more vicious than the last with a central immortal one. Cutting off a head only caused another to instantly grow in its place. A stealthy predator, it preyed upon the flocks of neighbouring farmland while its poisonous breath befouled all land, water and air around it. The Hydra was eventually slain by Hercules, with the help of his nephew Iolaos who branded the bleeding stumps before the new ones could regenerate. Together, they buried the final, raging immortal head under a great boulder before Hercules dipped his arrows in its venomous blood, saving them for future use.

Slaying the Lernaean Hydra was Hercules' second task for King Eurystheus. His twelfth and final task involved capturing another many-headed monster, **CERBERUS**, who guarded the entrance to Hades, the Underworld. A terrible beast, Cerberus was the brother of the Hydra and the Chimera (*see page 10*), born of Echinda and Typhon (*see page 48*). He had three wild-dog heads, snakes all over his back and a dragon's tail. Hercules wrestled Cerberus into submission before dragging him before Eurystheus and finally returning him to Hades.

Above: Hercules and the Hydra of Lerna. Below: Hercules and Cerberus, both by Nicolo
Van Aelst, 1608. Facing page: Hercules and Iolaos; Cerberus, from an antique Greek vase.

JINN
invisible beings

JINN or **GENII** are low ranking divinities, their name deriving from the Semitic root *jnn*, 'to conceal'. In Muslim and Arabic lore they dwell amongst ruined buildings, haunting and prowling unclean places and the deserted wilderness of the vast Arabic wastelands, like the lowliest example of their kind, the **GHOUL** (*see page 18*). The cosmographer Al-Qazwini [1203-1283] wrote of them: '*The Jinn are aerial animals, with transparent bodies, which can assume various forms*'. These invisible shape-shifting creatures eat, have children and die, and can sometimes resemble monsters and animals and even mimick or possess humans.

They are believed to materialise from a cloud-like substance, from which they can agitate and become invisible at will '*by a rapid extension or rarefaction of the particles which compose them*'. In Egypt, tall walls of sand caused by desert winds are said to be caused by passing Jinn in flight.

In the *Quran*, Allah creates five orders of such beings out of smokeless fire: **JÁN** (Weaklings), **JINN** (Social), **SHAYATIN** (Devils), **IFRIT** (Demons) and **MÁRID** (Rebels). Most of these peacefully co-exist with human beings, but the shayatin (devils) often have darker designs, and work under their satanic father and chief **IBLIS**, the first jinn to disobey Allah in jealous rage at the creation of man.

Left: The Sleeping Genie and the Lady, engraving by the Brothers Dalziel, c.1865, from the Arabian Nights Entertainments. The English lexicographer Edward William Lane [1801-1876] wrote of 'the Djinn': 'If good, they are generally resplendently handsome: if evil, horribly hideous'. The specimen shown here could be a NASNAS, *a creature spawned of a human and a demoniacal* SHIQQ.

Facing Page: The Genie Appears, watercolour by Edmund Dulac [1882-1953] from The Arabian Nights. Weaker jinn can be summoned or even captured by sorcerers with the assistance of recitations, rituals and scheming demons. The Genie in the famous story of Aladdin and the Magic Lamp is one such captured spirit.

Above: Three pages from the late 14th century Arabic Book of Wonders, showing: a demon king of the jinns; Zawba'a the demon king of Friday; and the black king of the djinns, Al-Malik al-Aswad.

LAMASSU AND MANTICORE

and other lion people

The **LAMASSU** is a hybrid mythological animal originating in Sumeria. It has a male human head, the wings of an eagle and the body of a lion or bull (*variants shown opposite and on page iv*). Pairs of these creatures were sculpted at colossal size in Assyrian times, flanking gateways into cities. The four animals (*Bull, Lion, Eagle* and *Human*) represented the four fixed signs of the zodiac (*Taurus, Leo, Scorpio* and *Aquarius*) right into the Christian period (*as Luke, Mark, John* and *Matthew*).

A female Lamassu is effectively a **SPHINX** (*see page 44*), although a Sphinx may also be shown wingless, much like a **MANTICORE** (*below*).

The prevalence of lion-people in the ancient world stretches back 4,000 years to the Egyptian Goddess **SEKHMET** (*see opposite*).

Around 450 BC, the Greek physician Ctesias reported the existence of a living lion man, the deadly Persian **MANTICORE**. Pliny quotes him:

'*Mantichora, hauing three ranks of teeth... with the face and eares of a man, with red eies, of colour sanguine, bodied like a lion, and hauing a taile armed with a sting like a Scorpion*'. [from *Natural History*, Book 8, 30.]

Only elephants are safe from manticores. However, Aelian [175–235] relates, '*Indians hunt the young of these animals while they are still without stings in their tails, which they then crush with a stone to prevent them from growing stings*'.

Above left: A human-headed winged lion-bodied Lamassu, from Nineveh, dated to c. 700 BC.
Above right: Statue of the Egyptian goddess Sekhmet, with the body of a woman and the head of a lioness. The daughter of Ra, she was both a warrior goddess and a goddess of healing.

Left, and facing page: Manticores. These creatures are sometimes equipped with deadly porcupine-like quills for taking down humans, their favourite prey. Manticores may actually be an early interpretation of man-eating tigers. These still roam India today, lying in wait deep in the very same caverns where the ever volatile Manticore is also said to reside.

Leviathan

and other sea monsters

Early mythologies frequently embody chaos in serpentine or dragon-like form. **LEVIATHAN**, meaning 'twisted in folds', was one such huge and powerful beast of the seas. The Book of Job describes how the creature '*maketh the deep boil like a pot*'. The serpent once aggressively encircled the world, but was eventually defeated by Yahweh (*see below*).

The Leviathan is synonymous with other sea serpents of ancient Near Eastern and Indo-European origin. The 13th century Norse *Prose Edda* recounts the legendary Norse **JÖRMUNGANDR**, or 'huge monster', also known as the Midgard ('World') Serpent, fighting with the god Thor. Much earlier Ugarit texts from c.1250BC describe

LOTAN ('coiled'), a seven-headed Semitic god of the deep, being over-whelmed by the great storm god Hadad-Ba'al. Syrian seals from c.1700 BC describe an even earlier serpent, **TÊMTUM**.

The murderous eight-legged **KRAKEN**, Old Norse *kraki*, 'unhealthy/twisted/cranky' (*see front page*) was an enormous sea monster which lived off the coast of Greenland (*see page i*).

Left: Fishing boat attacked by a giant squid, drawn by W. A. Cranston 1893. In recent years, video footage has been captured for the very first time of this notoriously elusive species.

Another famous sea monster from ancient Greek mythology was SCYLLA, *who had four eyes and six long snaky necks equipped with grisly heads, each with three rows of sharp shark's teeth. Her body consisted of twelve tentacle-like legs, six dog's heads around her waist and the tail of a cat. Scylla lived on one side of a narrow channel of water, opposite the deadly whirlpool Charybdis. In Homer's Odyssey, the hero Odysseus has to steer his boat between them.*

Facing Page: Yahweh defeating Leviathan, order overcoming chaos, engraving by Gustave Doré , 1865. Below: Sea serpent attacking a boat, from the Swedish cartographer Olaus Magnus [1490-1557].

MANDRAKES AND DRYADS
and other plant people

The **MANDRAKE** or **MANDRAGORA** plant is a low-growing perennial with attractive red berries found in the Mediterranean region of Southern Europe. A pretty and unassuming little plant, it is actually an all-poisonous member of the nightshade family, also known as **SATAN'S APPLE**. It contains delirium-inducing alkaloids, known for their hallucinogenic and local anaesthetic properties. Its weird roots can reach up to four-feet deep and eerily resemble a semi-human form. The mandrake was once believed to be full of animal life and consciousness. To pull one from the ground was to meet certain death, as the humanoid root screamed and thrashed, irate at being forced from its earthy abode, its cries being fatal to all who heard them.

Another type of hybrid plant-person is the **DRYAD**, from the Greek *drys*, 'oak'. In Greek mythology these were the supernaturally long-lived spirits of trees. A **HAMADRYAD** was a dryad that was tied to just one tree. They are also central to Western European Druidic lore. More recently, they have been adopted by fantasy writers, e.g. the **ENTS**, in J. R. R. Tolkien's *Lord of the Rings* cycle.

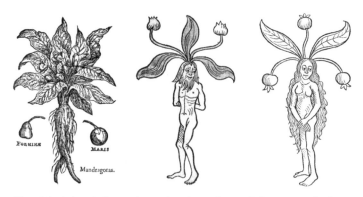

FOEMINÆ MARIS

Mandragoras.

Above: Mandrakes, also known since ancient times as 'love-apples', are strong aphrodisiacs.
Below: Dryads, or tree spirits. Illustration from Dante's Inferno by Gustave Doré, 1857.
Facing Page: The Ya-Te-Veo, or Madagascar tree, reputedly found in Africa, J. W. Buel, 1887.

MERMAIDS AND FISHMEN

and other fish people

With the upper naked body of a woman and the tail of a fish, **MERMAIDS** are beautiful yet soulless creatures who use their serene voices and ethereal beauty to bewitch crewmen, luring their ships onto rocks before dragging the terrified men down into the depths. They are closely related to the Greek **SIRENS** (*see page 24*).

In ancient Mesopotamia, c.3500 BC, **ENKI**, the Sumerian god of water and creation was depicted as a fish-man (*below right*), as was the later Assyro-Babylonian protector god **DAGON**, c.2500 BC (*opposite top left*), later known as **OANNES** by the Greeks, who also went on to honour the fish-god **POSEIDON** (the Roman **NEPTUNE**).

It was once common belief that every living thing existing on land had a counterpart in the sea, e.g. horses (sea-horse), lions (lion-fish), and dogs (dog-fish). In his *Natural History*, Pliny relates the discovery of the fossilized remains of a **TRITON** (a giant merman) unearthed in Joppa (modern day Tel Aviv) whose skeleton reached a monstrous 40 ft.

Some mermaid sightings may be mistaken glimpses of seals or of sea cows, such as Dugong.

Top left: the fish god Dagon, depicted on the ancient, sculptured walls of the palace of Dur-Sharrukin, present day Khorsabad. Top right: Mermaid and merman frolicking in the waves.
Below: Illustration from The Little Mermaid, by Hans Christian Anderson, 1836.

THE MINOTAUR
in the labyrinth

The offspring of Pasiphaë, Queen of Crete, and a majestic white bull sent to her by Poseidon, god of the sea, the dreaded **MINOTAUR** had the body of a man and the head of a bull, with the strength and tenacity to match. King Minos of Crete, determined to keep the monstrosity born of his wife secret, ordered the skilled craftsman Daedalus and his son Icarus to design a complex labyrinth to house the beast. The minotaur feasted ravenously on human flesh, and each seventh or ninth year, seven youths and seven maidens were sent from Athens as tribute and fed to the monster.

Eventually, the Minotaur was slain by Theseus, son of King Aegeus of Athens, with the assistance of King Minos' daughter, the beautiful Cretan princess Ariadne, who, madly in love with Theseus, obtained the secrets of the labyrinth from Daedalus and shared them with Theseus. She also gave him a long ball of thread, which allowed him to retrace his path and escape.

The name 'Minotaur' is derived from the Greek *Minos* and *tavros*, 'bull', forming the 'Bull of Minos'. The Minotaur's original birth name *Asterion* (named after King Minos's stepfather) means 'starry one', suggesting an association with the constellation Taurus.

*Above: Theseus and the Minotaur in the
Labyrinth, 1861 sketch by Edward Burne-Jones.
Theseus is shown carrying his father's sword
and holding the spindle of thread given him by
Ariadne. Left: The Minotaur at the centre of
the Labyrinth was a popular motif in Roman
mosaics, representing the tamed bestial nature
of the refined man. Facing page: Minotaur,
from a 450 BC Corinthian amphora.*

Nagas and Naiads

and other creation serpents

NAGAS, from the Sanskrit for 'cobra', are serpentine, semi-divine deities from Hindu mythology. Often depicted as human-headed snakes dwelling in treasure-laden palaces deep beneath the watery depths in the seventh ring of the netherworld, nagas can take on human form. Some female nagas, **NAGI** or **NAGINI**, have even married human men. To this day, some Hindu families claim descendance from nagas.

In early Hindu belief, a pair of serpent beings are responsible for man's very creation, under the rule of the great seven-hooded cosmic serpent **ANANTA SHESHA**. These guardians of treasures and esoteric knowledge sprang originally from the thousand eggs of Kadru, the wife of Kasyapa, the great Vedic sage of Hinduism. In Indian and Buddhist tradition, **VASUKI** is the serpent king, regarded in Asian mythology as being one of the 'Eight Great Dragon Kings'.

Serpent myths are widespread. In Chinese mythology, humans originate from a pair of male and female human-serpentine hybrids known as **FU XI** and **NU WA**, the offspring of the creation god Pangu (*opposite, lower right*). In Australian aboriginal myth, the **RAINBOW SERPENT** is a creator god who replenishes water holes, slithering between them as a rainbow or by forming gullies (*see below, after Danny Eastwood*). Other more playful types of water spirits include the ancient Greek **NAIADS**, female nymphs who presided over springs, wells, fountains, streams and rivers and the **NEREIDS**, sea nymphs (*see opposite*).

Above: Ananta Shesha, seven-headed creator naga-serpent, from an old Hindu engraving.

Above left: Naiads hidden in the waves. Right: The Chinese creators, Fu Xi and Nu Wa.

THE PHOENIX
and the fire salamander

The **PHOENIX**, also known as the **VERMILLION BIRD** (**ZHU QUE** in Chinese) or **FIREBIRD** (in Slavic folklore), has been the subject of many myths and beliefs since ancient times. Pliny the Elder writes:

'The phoenix ... is the size of an eagle. It is gold around the neck, its body is purple, and its tail is blue with some rose-coloured feathers.'

A phoenix can live for up to 500 years, at the end of which it prepares a nest of branches, resins and spices (including frankincense and cinnamon), before facing the sun to burst into flames, fanning the inferno with its colourful wings. According to Indian myth, a small maggot then emerges from the ashes, swelling daily in size and maturing to a fully-fledged phoenix after three days. Ancient Egyptian phoenixes, or **BENNU**, embalmed their parents' remains in package of myrrh and carried this to the Temple of Sun in Heliopolis for burial.

Another fire-loving creature, the **FIRE SALAMANDER** (*see below*) supposedly lived in fire and was reputedly so cold that it could extingish a blaze, causing stars to appear along its body. This may have originated in the fact that salamanders hibernate in rotting logs, so when logs were thrown on a fire, one of these lizards might 'appear'.

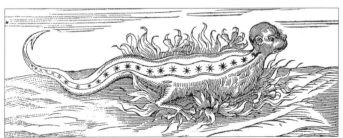

Phœnix

Above: Phoenix in the flames, from 1657.

Below: In Roman times the phoenix signified the longevity of the Roman empire. It has also been adopted as a Christian symbol of renewal, resurrection and immortality.

九嶷
九首人面鳥身居
此極天槉之山

Above: Woman riding a Ho-ho phoenix bird, Suzuki Harunobu, Japan, c.1750. In Japanese mythology the phoenix foretells of the coming of a new era.

Right: The 9-headed Chinese Fenghuang phoenix is one of the Four Spiritually Endowed creatures, Qing Dynasty.

THE SPHINX
Greek and Egyptian

The **ANDROSPHINX** (or man-sphinx) was widely depicted in Ancient Egypt around 1500 BC and featured a human head connected to a resting lion's body (*lower, opposite*). Entire avenues of such sphinxes still line and guard the approaches to tombs and temples to this day.

The Greek **SPHINX**, meanwhile, possesses the body and paws of a lion, the head and breasts of a woman, the wings of an eagle and sometimes a dragon's tail. She is believed to have hailed from either India or Ethiopia. According to Hesiod, she was the daughter of Echidna, fathered either by her son Orthrus, the two-headed dog, or the dragon Typhon (*see page 48*). In the c.450 BC story of *Oedipus and the Sphinx*, she guarded the entrace to the city of Thebes, lying in wait atop Mount Phikion for passers-by who she would seize and set a riddle on pain of death: "*Which creature has one voice and yet becomes four-footed, two-footed, and three-footed?*". No-one answered correctly until Oedipus, who replied: "*Man—who crawls on all fours as a baby, then walks on two feet as an adult, and then uses a walking stick in old age*". Furious at having her riddle solved, the Sphinx threw herself from the precipice.

A second, possibly more ancient, riddle is also recorded: "*There are two sisters: one gives birth to the other and she, in turn, gives birth to the first. Who are the two sisters?* Ans: Night and Day

Above left: Painted Etruscan perfume vase in the shape of a female sphinx, c.600 BC.
Above right: A Sphinx, from Attica, Greece, 540-530 BC, Metropolitan Museum of Art.

Facing page: Three different sphinx poses. From left to right: Crouching Theban or Greek sphinx; Passant guardian sphinx; Seated sphinx.

Left: Egyptian sphinx, c. 1500 BC. Egyptian sphinxes are typically wingless and male.

45

TROLLS
little and large

Old Norse wives' folklore tells of two kinds of **TROLLS**: giants (*jötnar*) and little people (*Huldrefolk*). The name 'troll' derives from the Middle High German *troll* (fiend) and *trolleri* (a creature which uses natural magic against humans to mischievous ends). Dwelling deep in the thick wild forests and murky dank caverns of Scandinavia, trolls lived simple yet brutish lives, and meeting one was to be avoided.

Primitive trolls were opportunistic hunters, kidnapping women and children from villages and pillaging and murdering wayfaring travellers on the roadside, a gruesome practice later shared by the cannibalistic Sawney Bean and his family, of historical Scottish legend.

They traditionally fashioned crude clubs from the surrounding trees and used huge boulders as weapons and missiles, many of which still litter the great mountain ranges of Sweden and Norway today. Especially large rocks are believed to be the bodies and final resting places of these giants, turned to stone by the sunlight.

Left: Troll by Jean No. Facing page: Trolls in the snow, by John Bauer [1882-1918]. Below: Mountain Troll, by Rolf Lidberg [1930-2005]. Trolls appear in the 13th century Norse Prose Edda and are often compared to Grendel, the rustic, supernatural enemy of Beowulf of Old English myth, and Hrungnir, the strongest giant of Norse mythology. Profoundly averse to noise, including lightning and the loud ringing of church bells from nearby villages, some milder-natured specimens also were also said to exist, more akin to Scottish brownies.

TYPHON

the terrible

The most dreadful creature in all mythology, **TYPHON** inspired terror in anyone who heard his name or witnessed his colossal bat-like wings spread against the moonlight. Hesiod tells of his fearsome appearance:

'From his shoulder grew a hundred serpents heads, a fearful dragon with dark flickering tongues, and from the eyes of his wonderous heads fires flashed beneath his brows and from all his heads fire burned as he glared'.

According to Hesiod, Typhon was the offspring of Gaia and Tartarus (the great abyss). The mythographer Apollodorus marvels that in size and strength he had no parallel, and that his body was 'All winged: unkempt hair streamed on the wind from his head and cheeks; and fire flashed through his eyes'. By Echidna, Typhon fathered many of the monsters of Classical mythology, the **HYDRA** (*p.26*), **CERBERUS** (*p.26*), the **GORGONS** (*p.20*), the **HARPIES** (*p.24*), the **CHIMERA** (*p.10*) and the **COLCHIAN DRAGON** (guardian of the Golden Fleece). From at least c.550 BC, Typhon was identified with **SET**, the Egyptian god of chaos and storms.

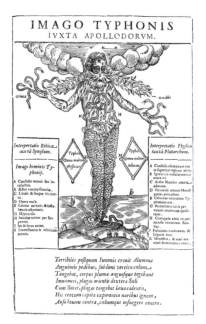

Above left: Typhon, by Athanasius Kircher, after Apollodorus, from Oedipus Aegyptiacus, 1653.
Above right: Alchemical depiction of Typhon as transmutation by Givanni Battista Nazari, 1589.

Left: Typhon, by Wenceslas Hollar [1607-1677], with two of his harpy children.

Facing page: The epic battle for supremecy between Zeus and Typhon was eventually won by Zeus, who threw thunderbolts and even the whole of Mount Etna at him. From an ancient Greek painting.

UNICORNS
and the hippocampus

Symbolising purity on every level, the **UNICORN** is a pure white horse with a single horn. Arab tradition relates how the unicorns of Ethiopia were *'ferocious beasts, impossible to capture'* except by setting a pure maiden within their sights. On seeing the young virgin, the unicorn would run to fall submissively at her feet, in turn becoming vulnerable to hunters. The unicorn was also adopted as a symbol of Christ

In Chinese mythology, the gentle **QILIN** (or **KI-LIN**) is a fabulous one-horned beast (*lower, opposite*), one of the 'Four Spiritually Endowed Creatures of the Five Elements'. Its appearance announces the birth or death of great figures, like Confucius or the Yellow Emperor.

In the 1700s, many sightings of unicorns were reported in Tibet. In 1820, a British Major Latta wrote home saying that he had seen one, and that they were known as the **TSO'PO** by the Tibetan locals. The emperor Genghis Kahn decided not to conquer India on the advice of a unicorn. Alexander the Great claimed to have ridden one!

Other magical horses include the winged horse **PEGASUS** (*p.21*) and the fabled **HIPPOCAMPUS** or **SEAHORSE**, a half-horse half-fish creature with webbed front legs which features in Phoenician, Etruscan, Pictish, Greek and Roman mythology (*shown below left, and right carrying a* **NERIED** *sea nymph*).

Oneger Aldro Wald Efil

Monoceros feu Vnicornu Zabatus Einhorn mit mahnen

Monoceros feu Vnicornu aliud. Einhorn mit mahnen ein ander art

Left: Origins of the Unicorn, or **MONOCEROS**, 'one-horn' as Pliny describes them. Dust from the horn could be used to detect poison, raise the dead and protect the dying, or to combat everything from the plague to epilepsy, bites from rabid dogs to the evil eye. Queen Elizabeth I owned two genuine unicorn horns, although these were probably the horns of narwhals (the 'unicorn of the sea'), which could reach up to two metres in length.

Below: Left: The **KI**, male Chinese unicorn. *Centre*: The **LIN**, female Chinese unicorn. *Right*: The King of the unicorns. From the ancient Ry Ya. In Buddist depictions, they are often shown walking on clouds or water, as they refuse to walk on grass for fear of harming a single blade. They are symbols of luck, protection, prosperity, success, fertility and longevity.

VAMPIRES
blood-sucking batmen

VAMPIRES originate in Slavonic myths in which the ghosts of criminals and heretics sucked blood from the jugular veins of people while they slept, transferring their vampirism on to their victims as they fed. Pieces of garlic and religious items such as holy water and crucifixes were used to deter attack. Sometimes a **DHAMPIR** was employed, a vampire's child with the useful ability to see invisible vampires.

In the 1700s, countless people died in a hysterical epidemic of vampirism in the Balkans, Poland and the Czech Republic. People were staked through the heart (with a hardwood stake, the best way to kill a vampire) and thrown half-dead into coffins (from which some tried to escape, creating yet more panic). The disease may have been cholera, as this too can produce sickly, pallid complexions, oversensitivity to sunlight, a gorged appearance and a ravenous thirst for blood.

Other similar beasts are: the deadly Puerto Rican **CHUPACABRA** (goat-sucker), the **CAMAZOTZ**, the cavernous bat-god of South America and the tropical blood- sucking **VAMPIRE BAT**.

Top left: Illustration from Carmilla, by Sheridan Le Fanu, the first vampire novel. 1872. Above: A typical vampire scene. Facing page: Vampire hunting in the 18th century. Lithograph by E. de Moraine. Left: Melusinian (serpentine) vampire, Paris, 1812.

The Dracula of Bram Stoker's famous Transylvanian story is based on cut-throat historical figures: Vlad the Impaler [1456-1476] and Countess Elizabeth Bathori [1560-1614]. Vlad was a bloodthirsty warlord, while the Countess was arrested in 1610 for the torture and murder of hundreds of girls and young women in order to bathe in baths of their blood – a ritual she believed essential to maintaining her youthful countenance.

WEREWOLVES AND ANUBIS
wolf men and the jackal man

The Old English term **WERWOLF**, 'man-wolf', invokes a wide range of human-animal transformations, including jaguars, bears and even crocodiles. Humans are made into werewolves either by enchantment, drinking from werewolf-populated watering holes or by being bitten by another. The werewolf roams under a full moon, with vulpine appetite, exhuming corpses and devouring infants and can only be killed with a silver arrow or specially blessed bullet.

The earliest example of these creatures is found in Greek mythology, when the Arcadian King **LYCAON** is transformed into a wolf by an angry Zeus (*see opposite*). A much earlier example of a jackal-man is the Egyptian god **ANUBIS** (*inset*), who ushered souls into the afterlife and guarded their graves.

Chinese and Slavic mythologies describe **LYCANTHROPY**. Herodotus writes that the Ukranian Neuri tribe turns into wolves once a year, possibly due to Shamanism. Pliny the Elder relates that a member of the Antaeus family transformed into wolfen form annually, across nine years: '*If he keeps himself from humans for this period of time, he returns... regains his form, except nine years of age have accumulated*'. In Mexican legend, a flesh-eating dog-like creature with a human hand growing from its tail was known as **AHUIZOTL**. It preyed upon village fisherman.

Above left: A medieval depiction of a werewolf, from the Nuremberg Chronicle, *1493.*
Above right: Aftermath of a werewolf attack, woodcut by Lucas Cranach the Elder, 1512.
Below: Lycaon, transformed into a wolf by Zeus, engraving by Hendrik Goltzius [1558-1617].

LIVING MYTHS
cryptozoological mysteries

Some mythological animals may be real living fossils. For example, stories of large, half-man, ape-like creatures remain soundly rooted in worldwide folklore. In Tibet there is the YETI (or YEH-THE or ABOMINABLE SNOWMAN, *opposite top*), which is resolutely reported by Sherpas to traipse the vast foothills of the Himalayas to this day. In North American there is the SASQUATCH (or YOSER or BIGFOOT).

Descriptions of these beasts worldwide are very similar—humanoid creatures covered with reddish-dark hair, reaching up to ten feet in height and weighing up to 800 pounds. Aggression, loud, resonant calls and an overwhelming odour are commonly reported by witnesses.

Another survivor from prehistoric times may be the Scottish LOCH NESS MONSTER. Tales of this animal, possibly a Plesiosaurus, date back to Saint Columba's sighting of it in the 6th century AD. And then there is the Australian BUNYIP, a leftover from the last Ice Age, which lurks in swamps, creeks, billabongs and waterholes (*see opposite*).

Above left: A Yeti, drawing by Vladimir Stankovic. Above right: An Australian Bunyip. Below & facing: Could a Plesiosaurus explain the Loch Ness Monster and Sea Monsters?

MODERN MYTHS

the explosion of fantasy

Modern mythological beasties have inhabited our imaginations ever since Mary Shelley wrote *Frankenstein* in 1818. Some fictions are fakes. In 1835, to boost sales, *The Sun* newspaper in New York reported that life had been discovered on the Moon by Sir John Herschel, a well-known astronomer of the time (*below*). More fantasies followed, such as H. G. Wells' 1898 *War of the Worlds*, Bob Kane's 1939 *Batman*, John Wyndham's 1951 *Day of The Triffids*, J. R. R. Tolkien's 1954 *Lord of the Rings* and J. K. Rowling's 1997 *Harry Potter*. Thus, the mythmaking continues ...

Entered according to Act of Congress, 1835 by Benj.H. Day   In the Office of the Clerk of District Ct of the United States for the Southern District of New York

LUNAR ANIMALS
AND OTHER
OBJECTS.
Discovered by Sir John Herschel in his Observatory at the Cape of Good Hope and copied from sketches in the Edinburgh Journal of Science.

For Description, See Pamphlet Published at this Sun Office